To,
Jen,

BALTIC DANCE

A MICHAEL QUINN SHORT STORY

KEVIN SCOTT OLSON

SOUTH POINTE PRESS

Baltic Dance - A Michael Quinn Short Story

First Edition

Ebook ISBN: 978-1-7324172-5-0

Print ISBN: 978-1-7324172-4-3

Edited and formatted by Ben Wolf

www.benwolf.com

Cover design by Book Covers Art

www.bookcoversart.com

Available in print and ebook format on amazon.com.

**Reviews for the international bestseller
Michael Quinn novel *Night of the Bonfire*:**

"Five stars, worthy of ten... grabs your attention and takes you for a wild ride!" - Goodreads review

"Loaded with action... Michael Quinn is ready for his own series." - Kirkus review

"Had me holding my breath and tensing with suspense... can't wait for more." - Amazon review

"A master writer... couldn't put down the book until I finished." - Amazon review

For more works by the author, visit
WWW.KEVINSCOTTOLSON.COM

The principal instrument of the Anglo-American is freedom; of the Russian, servitude. Their starting point is different, and their courses are not the same, yet each of them seems marked by the will of Heaven to sway the destinies of half the globe.

— ALEXIS DE TOCQUEVILLE

BALTIC DANCE

Late night
Berlin, Germany

THE ICY WIND OF MIDNIGHT SWEPT THE DESERTED
boulevard of *Eckestrasse,* tossing dust and scraps of trash in
mad little spirals.

Michael Quinn turned up the collar of his leather jacket as
he walked. The dingy sidewalks and concrete buildings of
Berlin, which could be those of any big city at night, had
earlier seemed cold and impassive. Now they were welcome.
The solitude calmed his nerves.

Walking back to his hotel gave him time to decompress
from the intensity of the last couple of hours. The chilly night
air was a welcome break from the smoke and noise of the bar.

In the thick fog that hung low from the sky, the yellow
street lamps looked like floating guideposts. *We will show you
the way*, they signaled, *so you can be alone with your thoughts.*

His assignment in Germany was done. After some tense

vetting, things had gone as planned. Less than a half-hour earlier, in one of the tawdry bars a few blocks behind him, he'd successfully handed off the flash drive. It contained information so sensitive that no amount of encryption would suffice to have it sent through any kind of electronic communication. It could only be delivered in person, to one person.

Trusted soul to trusted soul, the Director had ordered.

Mission accomplished. Now all Quinn wanted was to go home. The drab Berlin cityscape held no attraction for him. He hunched his shoulders against the wind.

"Hallo."

The faint, feminine voice seemed to come out of nowhere.

Quinn whirled around.

At the far end of the block, red taillights glimmered as a black car turned onto a side street. The lights disappeared, and the boulevard was again empty.

The voice had probably echoed from an open car window. Quinn put his hands back in his pockets and walked on, thinking of his hotel room's warm bed.

Something moved in the mist, ahead on his right.

"Ich mochte partei?"

A dark-haired girl emerged from a recessed doorway. She stepped toward him, her breath exhaling like cigarette smoke into the air.

He stopped, curious.

She wore black fishnet stockings, a black leather coat, and black high-heeled boots. The coat was pulled tight against her shapely figure. She flashed an inviting smile.

But her eyes betrayed her. Dark and soulless, they were set

deep in bony sockets. The yellow street lamp illuminated the gaunt, prematurely aged face of an addict.

Her skin was sickly pale, and her shoulder-length hair, lipstick, and long nails were all colored a funereal black. Both wrists bore leather bracelets with metal spikes. The tattoo on her neck, of a rose-covered coffin, completed the picture.

A German gothic working girl. Not a sub-culture Quinn cared to hang with this evening.

"*Nein danke, fraulein.*" He shook his head and walked on.

Footfalls echoed behind him. The gothic girl was following. His eyes narrowed as she reappeared alongside him, matching his pace. They passed the last fading lights of the clubs and bars.

"*Amerikaner?*"

"Yes."

"Frahm whar?" She switched to broken English.

"California."

"Ah, *Kalifornien.* Vill you take me zare?"

"It's late." Quinn ignored her attempt to make eye contact and continued walking. Now they were alone in an area of dark buildings.

"*Nein,* it is never late in Berlin,*"* the girl said in a faux-sultry voice. She linked her arm through his and pressed her body against him. The scent of her cheap perfume hung in the air.

Quinn extricated his arm and moved toward the street, his body tensing in case this was anything beyond what it appeared to be. A glance back showed no sign of anyone following them. The girl wanted one more score for the evening; that was all this was. He was about to tell her to go home when her hand took hold of his wrist.

She stopped, facing him. An alley with an overloaded dumpster was behind her.

Her free hand pulled at her belt, and her black leather coat opened, revealing alabaster-white breasts jutting out from a black leather bra. A silver navel ring glistened on her bare stomach. Her pierced tongue licked black lips as she tugged him closer.

Then her hand moved inside her coat pocket.

The ploy was beyond obvious. Quinn wrenched his wrist free and was braced and ready when a man dashed out from behind the dumpster. He focused on the knife in the man's hand. Then he startled at a sudden movement to his right.

"*Bastard!*" The girl spat the word and brandished a hypodermic needle and syringe taken from her coat pocket. She hissed something in German and waved the needle back and forth.

The man, powerfully built with a shaved head, charged Quinn while the girl moved nimbly to the side, as if choreographed. She jockeyed for position, looking for the moment to plunge the needle into his skin.

Quinn sidestepped and deflected the man's knife arm upward with his forearm, then jabbed his elbow hard into the man's face. The man grunted and tried to throw a counterpunch, but Quinn grabbed the wrist of the man's knife hand and, stepping forward, twisted it sharply toward the ground.

The man tripped and fell sideways, grabbing Quinn's jacket with his free hand. Quinn stumbled, and metal glinted to his right. The girl lunged at him, aiming the needle at his exposed neck.

His right leg shot out in a sidekick, and the steel cap of his shoe hit the girl's elbow. She shrieked, and her arm jerked up as she stumbled backward. The needle tumbled end-over-end through the air.

Quinn forced the man's arm down to the sidewalk. He stomped hard on the exposed wrist and heard the satisfying *crack* of breaking bone.

The man howled in pain and collapsed. His gloved hand opened and dropped the knife. Quinn heard footsteps and glimpsed the girl running away into the fog. He lifted the man by his shoulders and shoved him face-first against the dumpster.

The man grunted as his face collided with the rough-edged metal. He staggered, rubbing his face, and turned around, only to see Quinn's 9mm trained on him.

His face bleeding with cuts from the dumpster, the man spat and cursed something in German, then he darted down the alley and disappeared into the darkness.

———————

The next evening
Hotel Luxe Central lounge, Berlin

"THAT WAS QUITE THE COCKTAIL THAT YOUNG LADY HAD prepared for you, Michael." Dieter, Quinn's contact in Berlin, placed his cell phone on the bar as he slid onto the barstool next to him.

"I'm more of a Scotch man." Quinn nodded at his Glenfiddich on the rocks.

Dieter ordered a Dunkles beer from the bartender and then scrolled the cell phone screen until he came to a photograph of the hypodermic needle lying on some sort of examining table under bright fluorescent lights.

"That may have been your last drink of any kind, my friend." His voice was soft-spoken. "What a mix of pharmaceuticals she had in there. They were designed to loosen you up so you would happily explain in detail everything you knew about anything."

"They thought I knew the contents of the flash drive. What was in that syringe, scopolamine?"

"Something much more potent. I'm not privy to details, but I believe a psychoactive drug similar to the Russian serum SP-117. It was laced with other chemicals whose nature is still undetermined. When they were done with you, of course, they would have killed you. We might have found your body in that dumpster."

"Fortunately, goth girls have never been my type. Anything on her or her boyfriend?"

"Nothing. No prints on the knife, and no security cameras there. This incident will just be a footnote to a successful mission. Perhaps you will learn not to talk to strange girls in such a rough part of town, yes?"

"Duly noted." Quinn sipped his whiskey. "And I assure you I have no plans to return there. Instead, I'm going for a run on a beach and a swim in the Pacific. I'm booked on the 7 a.m. flight home to California tomorrow morning."

"Not anymore you're not. A new assignment has just come in. Your field supervisor Will texted me an hour ago."

"Something here in sunny Berlin?" Quinn kept his demeanor calm, but his heart rate jumped, as it always did, with the challenge of a new case.

"You get to freeze your ass off a bit farther north." Dieter flicked the screen to a picture of a wide, smooth-flowing river flanked by rows of three and four-story buildings, all with the architecture of old Europe.

Yet not quite Europe. A majestic structure topped with golden domes and tall spires drew Quinn's eye. "Russia?"

"St. Petersburg, to be exact. With a stop in what might be new territory for you."

Dieter flicked his cell phone screen to a map of Europe. He scrolled up, past Italy, France, and Austria, until, just north of Germany and Poland, the map centered on the blue waters of the Baltic Sea. To the left of the sea lay Sweden and Norway, and to the right stretched the vast expanse of Russia.

Dieter's finger traced three small countries that bordered the sea on one side and Russia on the other. "Ever been to the Baltic countries—Estonia, Latvia, Lithuania?"

"No."

Dieter's finger stopped on the middle country. "Your first stop is in Riga, Latvia's capital. And your mission concerns something more interesting than a flash drive."

Dieter flicked the screen again, and an official-looking photograph of a young woman appeared on the screen. She had light brown hair, a fair complexion, and striking eyes— gray with a touch of blue.

Her facial features might have been pretty, but Quinn

7

couldn't tell because of her grim countenance. Her eyes weren't deadened like those of the German goth girl, but they were wary. Her mouth was drawn in a thin straight line.

"Meet Karina Lusis. Twenty-seven years old, a Latvian national, lived there all her life. Five-foot-eight, one hundred twenty-five pounds. Graduate *summa cum laude* of the University of Latvia. A linguist by profession. Fluent in seven languages, including English."

Dieter zoomed in on the image. "And for the past three years, she has also been a junior operative in the *Drosibas Policija,* Latvia's counterintelligence service."

"She should smile more."

"She is certainly not smiling now. She was kidnapped by the Russians last night."

"Was she running an op?"

"Yes. Working undercover in the eastern part of Latvia, near the Russian border."

"Why was she kidnapped?"

Dieter drank from his beer and sat back. "Big picture, Russia is looking to regain its lost empire. Russia's success in seizing land in Crimea and Ukraine has emboldened them to cast their eye on the Baltics, which they ruled under the old Soviet Union.

"The Baltic countries, of course, treasure their independence. They want to be part of a prosperous Europe, not a vassal of a resurgent Russian empire. NATO is aware of this and has moved additional troops into northern Europe.

"Russia doesn't want to trigger a full-scale war with the NATO countries. So they are playing small-ball against the Baltics: harassment, military intimidation, and kidnapping."

"How will this kidnapping bring Russia more territory?"

"They are using their Crimea playbook: use operatives to agitate and create a phony disturbance, in this case in Latvia near the Russian border. When the time is right, Russia will then declare that a 'preventive occupation' is necessary to restore order."

"And Russian soldiers move in?"

"Yes. And a slice of Latvia is seized and declared part of Russia."

"It worked for Hitler with the Sudetenland." Quinn looked at the map of the small Baltic country. It looked about the size of Maine. "But why did Latvia send a linguist on a risky op like that?"

Dieter ran his hand through his hair. "She was chosen for the op because she speaks fluent Latgalian, the dialect in that part of Latvia. Things had gone well. She had successfully infiltrated the cell of agitators and was preparing a report to expose them when the Russians apparently learned who she was, kidnapped her, and hauled her across the border into Russia."

"Is she being held for ransom?"

"On a grand scale. The Russians say she will be released unharmed if Latvia will allow the Russian troops in for their 'preventive occupation.' But Latvia won't agree to give up a piece of its country in exchange for a hostage."

Dieter looked at the dark brown liquid in his glass. "The Russians have already arrested Karina on bogus charges of espionage. If Latvia doesn't agree to Russian demands, torture and interrogation await her, followed by a show trial in Moscow and certain conviction."

9

"Latvia's a member of NATO now. What about exerting pressure with conventional diplomacy?"

"A kidnapping like this doesn't rise anywhere close to the level of what the NATO pact considers an attack."

Quinn swirled the ice in his drink. "Pretty shrewd. But doing nothing isn't an option for us. Inaction from the West will only be interpreted by the Russians as a sign of weakness."

"Precisely. And it could lead them to believe the time is right for a larger invasion. Reclaiming one of the Baltics for the Russian empire would stun the world."

Dieter fell silent and gave Quinn a knowing glance. There was no need to spell out what had to be done.

"So, we have a hostage rescue situation." Quinn finished his drink and let the weight of his new assignment sink in. "Where is she being held, and by whom?"

Dieter flicked to the next image. "In a small commercial warehouse on the outskirts of St. Petersburg."

His screen showed a run-down industrial area full of aging buildings and warehouses. He zoomed in on a one-story building with a single door in front and a roll-up steel garage door in the back.

Dieter opened another file. His face hardened as a photo of a man's face filled the screen. "Her kidnapper is a piece of work. Venedikt Kusnetsov. Former member of Spetzgruppa A of the FSB Special Purpose Forces."

"Former?" Quinn took in the man's hawk nose and the smallish brown eyes that stared back at the photographer. The man was in his mid-thirties, with a clean-shaven head and goatee that vaguely resembled Lenin.

"Yes. Drummed out of the special forces for sadistic cruelty."

"That shouldn't bother the Spetznatz. They're trained in bullying and beating."

"Yes, but Kusnetsov took it to another level. The FSB wants its operatives to kill as efficiently as possible and get out of there. Kusnetsov's modus operandi is torture. Not only on his enemies but anyone whom he felt crossed him. He prefers long, slow work with surgical instruments."

"Nice guy." Quinn scrutinized the photo and noted a faint half-inch scar above Kusnetsov's left eyebrow.

"Moscow keeps him at arms' length, sub-contracting him out for jobs such as this where his cruelty is an advantage." Dieter sipped his beer. "He's got three henchmen with him on this job. Two outside, guarding the building, and one with him, inside the building. You will need to neutralize all of them. The world will be a better place with them gone."

"What timeframe are we dealing with?" Quinn's jaw tightened. This wasn't going to be pretty.

Dieter tapped his fingers on the bar counter. "The Latvian government is stalling for time, and the girl is said to be unharmed, so far. However, as soon as Moscow decides Latvia is not serious—a couple of days, perhaps—they will give Kusnetsov the go-ahead to begin his torture."

"Dieter, you know that a hostage rescue like this usually requires a team of about twenty men. There'd be a perimeter team, an entry team, an intel specialist, a couple of snipers…"

"Michael, we can't run the risk. If things go wrong, it could literally mean war between nations. Russia is looking for any excuse to move troops in. And, we know you prefer to

11

plan your own op and work alone. We will get you there and outfit you with whatever equipment you need. The rest of the op is in your hands."

"I'll make do. But just how do you propose to get me the 700 miles into St. Petersburg?"

A smile crossed Dieter's face. "You'll like this route." He glanced at an empty table in a dark corner. The bar area was getting crowded. "Let's move to that corner table and order another round of drinks."

Two hours later, Dieter sighed and sat back in his chair. His soft-spoken voice was tired and hoarse. "Okay, my friend, I think you are good to go. The op you are planning is, as expected, outlandish."

"And it just might work."

The next morning
Riga, Latvia

QUINN STEPPED OUT OF HIS TAXI ONTO THE cobblestone street of *Elizabetes iela* and was greeted by the delicious smells of fresh-baked pastries and dark-roast coffee.

His senses were tuned to soak up the first impressions of the new country. He'd kept his expectations low, preparing himself for a bleak land marred by poverty and the scars of its Soviet occupation.

To his pleasant surprise, he found himself strolling along the sunny, tree-lined streets of Old Town, an area as charming as any village in Switzerland or Austria. Friendly cafes and shops invited visitors to linger. The architecture was an attractive mix of old Europe, ranging from medieval to Art Noveau.

On the flight from Berlin, he had received the latest intel about the kidnapping of Karina, now well on the path to becoming an international incident. The Latvian government, displaying polite outrage, had sent several diplomatic notes to the Russian Ministry of Foreign Affairs.

Russia had not deigned to send a response. The Latvian government had then made "urgent" appeals to the European Union, the European Council, and the upcoming United Nations Human Rights Council meeting in Geneva.

Good luck with all that. Quinn walked toward the Old Town Bakery, the source of the wonderful aromas. *Perhaps type the next diplomatic note in capital letters.*

Bells hanging from a ribbon jangled as he entered the bakery.

Two young couples chatted at the back of the small establishment. An elderly, gray-haired woman sat at a front table. She was having her morning coffee and reading *The Baltic Times.* Her black and white coat was draped on the chair next to her.

Quinn greeted the pony-tailed waitress behind the glass display case and examined the savory display of Danishes, chocolate eclairs, and cupcakes. He settled on a slice of *Klingeris*—a type of coffee cake—and black coffee.

He sat at the counter and people-watched as he drank his coffee and consumed the delicious golden cake. It was a clear, blue-skied morning, and many locals rode bicycles or walked to their destination.

Quinn glanced up at a mirror hanging over a polished

espresso machine. Behind him, the old woman sipped her coffee and turned to page four of the *Times*.

Black and white coat on the chair, and page four of the newspaper. She was his contact, and the meeting was on. Some tools of his trade were impervious to technology.

He left the bakery and walked a block and half to a picturesque local park. Tall, shady trees bordered tidy lawns and flowerbeds of yellow and white daisies. Old men sat on benches while laughter echoed from a children's playground.

In the center of the park, a small wooden bridge curved over a winding stream. Quinn walked to the top of the bridge and waited, wondering about the dozens of padlocks affixed randomly to the bridge handrails. Many of the padlocks had brightly colored initials and hearts painted on them.

"Welcome to the Baltics, Mr. Quinn."

The old woman from the bakery appeared on his right, her tote bag and coat draped over one arm. Up close, her weathered, craggy face conveyed a dour expression.

She reached into her bag and removed a manila envelope. "Helena, at your service. Your papers are all here and in order. Passport, ship ID, even an itinerary of your cruise."

The woman spoke with crisp efficiency as Quinn examined the contents. "Per your instructions, your cover is as Mr. Justin Ridgeway, a prosperous American real estate investor, now a tourist on a luxury cruise to the Baltics and Russia."

"Looks like I've done pretty well for myself."

Helena looked like she'd been born with that stern look on her face. She nodded but did not acknowledge his attempt at humor. "Your suitcase is already on board. The other arrangements you requested have also been made."

She removed her cell phone from her bag and shielded it from the sun as she showed him a photo of a brown-haired thirtyish man with a mustache.

"This is Anton, your driver in St. Petersburg. He will meet you on a street near the dock, holding a sign with 'Ridgeway' hand-lettered on it. He will be driving a black Mercedes sedan.

"Anton has worked for us for some time and is completely trustworthy. For our purposes here, however, he is on a need-to-know basis. He has been instructed to take you to the safe house, to the point of extraction, to wherever you say, without asking questions. Beyond that, he knows nothing. We would appreciate it if you involve him as little as possible."

"Understood."

"Now, to our operative Karina." The old woman removed another manila envelope from her tote bag.

"She, of course, has no way to communicate with us, but I can give you a password that will let her know you are an ally sent to help her. When you first see her, you are to say 'It's a nice evening' in Latvian. Repeat after me: *Ta sirs skaists vakars.*"

Quinn did so, twice.

The woman nodded her head in satisfaction. "And she will reply, 'Unless it rains,' in Latvian, as follows: *Kad nau lietus.*"

Quinn repeated that as well.

"Good. Please use the password with your driver, as well. Be careful of conversation with anyone else. If you get into trouble with the authorities in Russia, we cannot help you."

Quinn thought of the map showing the tiny country and its belligerent neighbor. "I imagine there are times when you would just as soon land a division of Latvian troops in Russia and stop all this."

Helena gave him a sharp glance. She wore no makeup and, by her appearance, had long ago ceased caring whether the world noticed her age spots and homely features. In the sunlight, she could have been Mother Time, with a thousand lines etched deep in her face. Her shoulders sagged with the weight of many sorrows.

But when she spoke, her words showed a mind very much engaged.

"Of course we would. But that is exactly what the Russians desire. They would then claim to be the invaded country. And by the end of that day, my country, the Republic of Latvia, would no longer exist."

She gestured with pride at the well-kept trees and flowers of the little park.

"In this part of the world, Mr. Quinn, the dance with the Russians is done differently. We must take care with each dance step.

"Your United States was blessed to be born in freedom. My country has known independence for less than thirty years. Before that, we were conquered by the Russians, before that the Nazis, and prior to that the Russians again.

"Beyond our borders lies constant danger. We cherish our liberty dearly, and—" her voice rose, "—we do not wish to be devoured by the Russian bear again."

She opened her mouth as if to continue, then she licked her lips and handed Quinn the envelope. "But this is not the subject for today. This envelope has Karina's papers; please examine them. Your ship, the *Sea Goddess,* begins boarding at 2pm. Is there anything else?"

Quinn felt the need to lighten her mood. "One thing. I'm curious about all these padlocks on this little wooden bridge. They have hearts, initials, little messages painted on them in bright colors. What are they all about?"

Helena's face creased into a smile. Her eyes moistened as she gazed at the array of locks adorning the bridge. "We are on Love Lock Bridge. It is an old tradition here in my country. Young lovers come here when they get engaged. They paint their name or initials on a lock, lock the padlock on the bridge, and throw the key in the water because they are to be married forever."

Quinn opened the envelope and looked at Karina's passport. It was in the name of Mrs. Jessica Ridgeway.

Helena extended a wrinkled hand. "Good-bye, Mr. Quinn. I imagine that this is your first mission in which your assignment is to rescue your wife."

The next evening
St. Petersburg, Russia

THE *SEA GODDESS* GLIDED THROUGH THE CALM WATERS OF the Neva River, moonlight shining on its wake of white froth.

The cruise ship's journey across the Baltic Sea, through the Gulf of Finland, and up the river had gone according to schedule. With the busy commercial traffic of the day gone, the elegant white ship had the river to itself.

Quinn stood on the top deck, happy to be away from the crowds that mingled below on the restaurant and lounge decks. It was a cool, clear night, and in the coal-black sky, countless stars shone in brilliant silver and white. These were the same distant points of light that had greeted seafarers hundreds of years ago, thousands of years ago. They would be there a thousand years from tonight.

He sipped his whiskey and watched the ship slowly pull into port.

Past a golden-spired cathedral, through an open drawbridge lit in turquoise, the lights of St. Petersburg shimmered on the river like those of a beautiful underwater city.

What history that river had witnessed!

The magnificent Winter Palace came into view, its green and white baroque architecture bathed in amber light. Inside those Palace walls, Catherine the Great had dreamed of bringing her country into the modern era.

Inspired by the Enlightenment sweeping Europe, she founded universities and the Hermitage. She encouraged businesses to prosper with Adam Smith's ideas on capitalism, and she encouraged the arts by importing French plays and Italian opera. Her goal was nothing less than to develop her beloved Russia into a flourishing part of Western civilization.

But it was not to be. Russian history became a bloody and violent three steps forward, two steps back, culminating in the twentieth-century abyss of the Soviet Union.

Quinn watched the city lights grow closer. What if Catherine the Great's dream had come true? Then there might have been no World War I, no Bolshevik Revolution. No gulag, no Soviet empire.

Maybe no Kusnetsov to deal with tonight.

The ship's engines growled, and then Quinn felt a gentle bump. The ship was docking.

He glanced down at his crisply pressed slacks. Tonight was "formal night" on the ship, and he was appropriately dressed in black pants, a white tuxedo coat, a white shirt, and a black bow tie. His lips pursed at the contrast between his clothes and his actual plans for "formal night." He finished his drink and tossed the plastic cup in the trash as he went downstairs to join the disembarking passengers.

Tourists from several ships crowded the dock, off for an evening at the ballet, the opera, or the many restaurants along the glittering main boulevard of Nevsky Prospect. The crowd thinned as he walked a half block in the chilly night air to a darkened area, toward a man waiting in front of an idling Mercedes. The man held a hand-lettered sign that said, "Ridgeway."

"*Ta sirs skaists vakars,*" said Quinn.

"*Kad nau lietus,*" replied Anton the driver. He nodded and opened the back door of the Mercedes.

After perfunctory greetings, the ten-minute drive passed in silence. The safe house was a duplex at the end of a quiet cul-de-sac. Anton drove the car into the garage, closed the garage door, then motioned for Quinn to exit.

Up a cramped staircase, they walked into the living room of a modest two-bedroom apartment with the blinds drawn. Quinn's clothes and gear lay neatly on one of the beds. As he undressed and carefully laid out his evening clothes on the bed —he would be wearing them again—he glanced into the other bedroom.

On the other bed, also carefully arranged, lay a formal evening gown, shoes, and underclothing, all in Karina's size. Everything he had asked for was there, even the jewelry and a makeup kit.

In five minutes, he was dressed, head to toe, in black clothing. In addition to being non-reflective, the clothing also blocked infrared technology and was thus invisible to most night-vision cameras.

He took care, as he always did, with his gear. He strapped on his hip holster and drew his HK 9mm three times to make sure it didn't catch.

Next came his body-armor assault vest. Inside the vest pockets, he found the knife and spare magazines he'd requested. He put on the vest, packed the rest of his gear into a backpack, and adjusted the straps.

Last was the heavy artillery. He picked up the HK MP5 9mm rifle from the bed. It came, also as requested, with a suppressor and two attached 30-round magazines, clipped so he could quickly change magazines. The ammo was subsonic hollow-point, to minimize noise. He adjusted the rifle sling. Ready to go.

The drive to the target area also passed in silence. They entered an area of older industrial buildings and dark, empty streets. Anton dropped him off in an unlit alley two blocks from the target building, then the Mercedes purred off into the night.

Quinn looked around. The change in his surroundings was surreal. He was alone in a very different world from the bright lights and crowds of Nevsky Prospect.

This industrial area was even more run down than in the

photographs. The dilapidated buildings and warehouses that lined the alley looked to be from Soviet days. Some of the buildings were boarded up, and others looked abandoned.

The only sound was the din of the city, a faint roar of distant traffic and voices that sounded oddly like the ocean. As Quinn walked down the alley the sound was enough to cover his footsteps, as long as his boots avoided broken glass and metal scraps.

He saw no signs of life. Any business that could afford to move to greener pastures had long ago moved on. Neighborhoods, like humans, can grow sick and die. This was a dying neighborhood. The symptoms were its blight and decay.

Low clouds had moved in, shrouding the moon, and the resulting darkness was Quinn's friend. Most of the streetlights were out, either from lack of maintenance or from being shot out by vandals.

He stopped at the end of the alley, a block from his target. His breath formed white plumes in the chilly air. The temperature was dropping as the Russian night settled in. Gusts of wind swept down the alley, biting through his clothing.

What would he do if a police car turned the corner and lit him up with its headlights? He hadn't bothered with a cover story. Armed as he was, there was no plausible cover story.

Keeping close to the buildings, he made his way along the block until the target building was in sight across the street. As the photos had shown, it sat on a street corner. And it bore the only sign of life in the area: light shone from a small, barred window, blinds drawn, and from a skylight on the roof.

He found a recessed doorway that offered a full view of the building side that paralleled the street and a partial view of the rear of the building. He pressed into the back corner of the doorway and removed his night-vision binoculars from his backpack.

The one-story building looked just as drab bathed in green light. Brighter green light shone from the window and skylight. Somewhere at the front of the building was the guard stationed at the entrance. And somewhere else, also out of Quinn's sight, was the second guard, the roamer.

The building, he'd been assured, had no motion sensors or cameras. It was not barricaded, and there were no attack dogs, not even an alarm system. The kidnappers were confident in the obscurity of their location.

He looked at his watch and set the chronograph to count-down. Assuming the ship left St. Petersburg on schedule later tonight, he now had just under ninety minutes to complete the op.

He waited, shivering in the night air.

A green human shape carrying an AK-47 rounded the far rear corner of the building. The roamer.

The man walked at a slow pace along the back of the building, then turned and walked along the street side, away from Quinn. As he walked, the roamer's head turned from side to side, scanning the area. He stopped, spoke briefly into his cell phone, and then resumed his patrol.

Quinn used the binoculars to map out a clear path to jog across the street, then he tucked them in his backpack. At close range, the ambient light would be sufficient.

His fingers ran over his rifle and sling and moved it from his front to his side. He touched his holstered 9mm and tested his backpack straps. Finally, he gripped the textured handle of the stiletto-shaped six-inch knife hanging handle down, its blade sheathed, in a pocket in the upper front of his assault vest.

The roamer rounded the far rear corner again, walked along the back of the building, then turned the corner and started down the street side.

Quinn fast-walked across the narrow street, his footsteps silent. He slowed his pace as he turned and crept along the sidewalk directly behind the roamer. He unsheathed the knife.

The roamer's silhouette came into focus as Quinn closed in, now just a few steps behind. The roamer's head swiveled from left to right. The thick back of his neck offered itself.

In one motion, Quinn grabbed the roamer and pulled him close, clamped his hand over the roamer's mouth, and plunged the knife into the side of the roamer's neck and then forward. The roamer jerked and gurgled, and then blood spurted and his body went limp as the blade severed the carotids, bringing instant unconsciousness.

Quinn laid the roamer's lifeless body down on the concrete, wiped the blood off the knife, and hurried to the front of the building. He stopped and peered around the corner.

The entry guard was sitting in a folding chair, his back to Quinn. His AK-47 lay on the ground next to him. He held a lighter in one hand and a cigarette in the other. The man leaned back in his chair and brought the cigarette and lighter up toward his mouth.

The guard's arms jerked and eyes bulged as a hand covered his mouth and jerked his head back. The guard grunted as the knife blade plunged into the side of his neck. His legs kicked out and he made one feeble effort to rise, and then he slumped back in his chair, blood pooling on his chest. Both of his hands opened, and the cigarette and lighter dropped to the ground.

Quinn arranged the body with his head down and his hands on the lap so that from a distance it looked like the guard was resting in his chair or perhaps had nodded off.

He looked at his watch. Ten minutes had elapsed. How long until the roamer was due to check in again?

Get on with it. From his backpack, he withdrew the olive-colored plastic package that contained the door charge.

With a hostage situation, he didn't have the luxury of making a statement by blowing half the building in. The charge needed to be powerful enough to blast open the door but not so powerful as to hurl metal fragments that could harm the hostage.

Quinn had estimated the necessary explosive force of the charge based on Dieter's photographs of the front door. He unwrapped the package, removed the adhesive strip on the back, placed the charge on the door lock, and capped the charge.

Careful with each footstep, he padded around to the windowless side of the building, placed a second, smaller charge against the circuit breaker box, and capped it.

The light from the roof showed him the position of the skylight, his point of entry. He put down his backpack and removed the lightweight, telescoping ladder strapped to its frame. The ladder was small, but its carbon fiber composite would bear his weight, and its sixteen-foot reach would get him onto the roof.

He pressed the side button, and the ladder quietly extended to its full length. Then he leaned the ladder against the building, put on his backpack, and climbed.

The roof was flat and made of inexpensive composition material. He put one foot on it to test his weight, then rolled the rest of his body onto the roof's sandpaper-like surface, keeping his profile as low as possible.

On the rooftop, the distant golden lights of St. Petersburg glimmered through the clouds. Winds were stronger, gusting from all sides, trying to chill his bones. But their added noise would help cover any sounds he might make, as would the sound-deadening composition surface, with no concrete tiles to shift or wooden shakes to crack. He kept his head down and crawled to the rear edge of the skylight.

A thick eyebolt protruding from the roof caught his eye. He tugged at it, found it sturdy, then removed a coil of rope from his backpack and tied one end to it. He raised his head and looked through the skylight.

His heart thumped at the sight of the three figures in the center of the room. The harsh fluorescent ceiling lights illuminated them so clearly, it seemed Quinn could reach out and touch them.

All had their backs to him. The girl, in a white blouse and jeans, sat in a metal folding chair. Her hands were bound behind her back, her ankles were tethered to the chair, and her mouth was gagged. Her blouse was partially unbuttoned and pushed down past the bra strap that ran across her back. Her pale shoulders and upper back showed no cuts or bleeding.

The inside guard stood in front of the girl. His head and neck were outside Quinn's field of vision, but Quinn could see the back and lower body of a stocky man dressed in a black coat and pants, holding an AK-47.

The guard turned to face the front door. Was he about to open it, to relieve the guard at the entrance?

To the right of the girl stood Kusnetsov.

Short and wiry, he wore a black tee-shirt and black pants. His shaved head glistened with perspiration. The butt of his 9mm protruded from his side holster. He turned to look at the girl, and Quinn confirmed his hawk-nosed profile and the small scar.

Next to the girl stood a small, stainless steel table holding a scalpel, a pair of needle-nose pliers, and a black taser with a pistol grip. The tools looked clean and unused, with no scraps of tissue or streaks of blood anywhere.

Quinn leaned forward and touched the skylight. It was, thankfully, glass, not plexiglass or the bullet-resistant acrylic used in modern structures. This glass would shatter easily. There was a danger that falling shards could harm the girl, but that had to be measured against the danger she was already in.

He punched in a code on his cell phone, watched the encrypted icon appear, and lay the phone on the roof.

He retrieved his fusion goggles from a zippered compartment in his backpack. Night-vision goggles with a thermal overlay, they amplified both the available light and thermal signatures. The orange outline of the thermal image would show anything that produced heat.

When Quinn slipped them on, they bathed the warehouse in the same green light as from his binoculars, but the three human shapes now burned in bright orange.

The wind picked up, sweeping across the rooftop and

rattling the vents. Quinn's chronograph showed he had seventy-one minutes left. His accelerating heart rate and increased blood flow told him it was crunch-time.

He leaned forward, took a knee, and aimed his rifle at the armed guard. While this exposed him, shooting down into the glass made for a more accurate hit. Then he could resume a prone position to take out Kusnetsov.

Quinn inhaled a deep breath and pressed the icon on his phone.

A double *bang* echoed around the building as the charges exploded, and the lights went out in the warehouse. The three orange-lit figures inside startled and looked at a small cloud of dust that spread inward from the front door.

Kusnetsov shouted something, and the guard stepped forward and aimed his AK-47 at the door.

Quinn fired a half-dozen rounds at the orange-lit guard. The skylight shattered as if hit by a giant hammer, and the piercing crash echoed through the night air as jagged shards fell straight down.

Kusnetsov dodged to the side and looked up. Quinn felt the man's cold eyes focus on him.

The guard stumbled as he was hit, but he didn't fall. He turned around and aimed his rifle up at the hole where the skylight used to be.

Quinn rolled to his side as the guard fired a stream of bullets across the skylight opening, shattering most of the remaining glass. As tiny glass shards fell to the roof, he cursed his realization that the guard was wearing a body-armor vest under his coat and was probably only wounded in the leg.

Staying just out of sight, Quinn turned on his side to look

through the opening. The warehouse was dark, but the fusion goggles showed the bright orange thermal outline of the three humans inside.

Kusnetsov brandished his 9mm and shouted something in Russian. The guard limped to the center of the room, aiming his rifle up at the skylight.

Quinn leaned in and fired a burst directly at the guard's head and chest. The rounds hit home, and the guard screamed and dropped his rifle, but Quinn had to duck away again as bullets from Kusnetsov's pistol hammered into the metal edge of the skylight and the roof. Quinn rolled farther away from the skylight, but more bullets tore through the roof around him.

Kusnetsov was following the sound of his movement.

Quinn froze in place and the gunfire ceased. He carefully rolled onto his stomach. With his weight on his elbows and toes, he lifted his body off the roof and slowly worm-crawled, making a wide arc around the skylight, toward the other side of the opening.

At any moment he expected bullets to rip through the roof and into his body, but the warehouse remained silent as he finished the painful crawl. His arm and back muscles burned as he maneuvered into an awkward position where he was still out of sight but could see the girl in her chair and the body of the dead guard on the floor.

But Kusnetsov was nowhere to be seen.

Quinn could see most of the green-lit warehouse, except for the front entrance and the corners. Was Kusnetsov crouching in one of those corners, texting for reinforcements?

He didn't see the telltale orange heat signature coming from any of them.

His heart hammered his breastbone as precious seconds ticked by. Winds whipped at his face. This was a hell of a time for a standoff. Why hadn't Kusnetsov fired? Was he low on bullets?

The chronograph read fifty-eight minutes left. Time was running out. Quinn leaned farther into the skylight opening so he could see the entrance.

The warehouse stayed silent.

Beyond the girl and the dead guard, he could see the front door a few inches ajar, its frame bent from the blast. If Kusnetsov had escaped, the door would be opened farther, and Quinn would have heard the sound of running footsteps.

He's still in the freaking building.

The thermal images were fuzzy, and the dead guard had a blurry outline of ghostlike orange light around his body. His heavy-set body lay on its side, the AK-47 rifle lying against its gut. Cold winds swirled in from the open door and skylight. As the warmth of the guard's body decreased, the orange thermal image faded as well.

But the orange outline at the top side of the guard's body seemed a brighter orange than the rest of the body.

There.

Something small and bright orange snaked across the guard's torso. Blood?

No. It was a human hand.

Quinn shifted his rifle into position.

You're a wily son of a bitch, Kusnetsov. He must've seen

29

Quinn's goggles, and was hiding in the one safe place: beneath the propped-up body of the dead guard.

And if Kusnetsov got hold of the guard's AK-47, he could blast Quinn off of the roof.

Kusnetsov's bright orange hand reached for the AK-47's pistol grip. Quinn leaned into the skylight opening and fired three rounds directly at the hand.

A shriek came from behind the guard's body, the hand jerked up, and then the guard's body rolled forward onto its stomach, exposing Kusnetsov's upper torso.

Quinn fired three shots at Kusnetsov's head and three into his chest. Orange bits and mist burst into the air, and Kusnetsov collapsed next to the dead guard.

The two bodies lay still. To a casual observer, they may have appeared asleep, except that fragments of Kusnetsov's brain lay splattered across the floor, and blood pooled from his chest onto the guard's corpse.

Quinn took a breath and removed the fusion goggles. He brushed bits of shattered glass off his phone and put it back in his pocket. From his backpack, he removed a steel carabiner, shaped like a figure eight with a larger loop at one end, and clipped the bigger loop to his webbed belt. Icy winds nipped at his fingers as he reached over to the coiled rope, secured the rope to the carabiner, and clipped the small loop to his belt.

He knocked out a remaining piece of skylight glass with his boot, perched on the edge, and rappelled down onto the warehouse floor. In seconds, his boots touched the floor, and he released the rope.

The woman watched, wide-eyed, as he walked over, his boots crunching in the broken glass. He cut the zip-ties binding her wrists and feet to the chair and removed her gag. Next, he produced a bottle of water from his backpack and handed it to her as he crouched in front of her, smiled, and spoke.

"*Ta sirs skaists vakars.*"

"*Kad nau lietus.*" Her voice came out as a croak, and she gratefully drank from the bottle of water. "And I speak English."

"Karina Lusis?" He punched buttons on his cell phone.

She nodded and took another drink of water. "American?"

"Yes, ma'am. Here to get you out."

"How?"

"A car is on its way to pick us up. Are you okay? Did they harm you?" He pulled her blouse back up over her shoulders and helped her stand.

"They slapped me a few times and made obscene threats about what they were going to do, the pigs. But I am unharmed. I've been kept sitting here. They were waiting for some sort of message. Permission, I think, from their superiors."

He was prepared for her to be paralyzed with fear or on the edge of hysteria. Instead, she seemed alert and quick-witted. She rubbed her arms to restore circulation and looked with disgust at the carnage on the floor.

Quinn's phone vibrated with the text message that the car was waiting by the side of the building.

She looked up at the hole in the ceiling where the skylight used to be. "How—"

"Come with me. I'll explain in the car."

31

ANTON EXPERTLY USED DARK SIDE STREETS TO TAKE THEM back into the city. Only when they crossed a major intersection did they get a glimpse, blocks away, of the bright lights and bustling crowds of the tourist areas.

They sat in the back seat. Quinn introduced himself and gave Karina a need-to-know explanation of who he was and the safe house where they were headed.

She listened intently, drinking from the bottle of water. In the shadowy light, she looked pale, thin, and wary, just like her photo. He watched for signs of shock, but her speech and body language showed her to be alert and composed.

"And what is plan after safe house, Mr. Michael Quinn?"

"We're going to get you home to Latvia."

"How? We are in Russia. The police will be looking everywhere for us. There will be roadblocks, helicopters." Her gray eyes flashed concern.

Quinn glanced at the city lights as they passed an intersection. She was right, of course. All hell would break loose as soon as Kusnetsov failed to check in. But Quinn had to keep her calm.

He explained, in a matter-of-fact tone, about the fake passports and papers, the evening clothes waiting for them at the safe house, and the cruise ship that was soon departing from St. Petersburg and headed to Latvia.

Her eyes widened as he spoke.

He ended lamely with, "So you see, all you have to do is memorize your name on your passport, and stay with me."

The Mercedes rounded a corner and pulled into the dark

cul-de-sac with the safe house. Karina looked out the window as they pulled into the driveway and then fired off a burst of anxious Latvian at the driver.

Anton responded with his own torrent of agitated Latvian, and, as he waited while the garage door opened, threw his arms in the air in a what-can-I-do gesture. After Anton finished, Karina looked at Quinn.

"This driver says all he knows is that you are highly regarded in your profession and that you know what you are doing." The garage door closed behind their car. "But to me, it seems, still great risk. You are sure this is best way?"

"Yes. Let's go upstairs, get changed, and get to our ship. You have a formal evening to attend."

THE BLACK MERCEDES SEDAN LOOKED COMMONPLACE AS it pulled in among the Bentleys, Rolls-Royces, and limousines double-parked next to the dock. Passengers from several luxury cruise ships were returning from their evening out, and the crowds mingled happily as they waited to board, drinking cocktails and chatting about the theater and the sights they had seen.

Some in the crowd might have wondered about the high-profile police presence. A line of police cars, their light bars flashing blue and red, sat parked in the center of the dock. Previous visitors to St. Petersburg may have been curious why the dock itself was now so brightly lit and why so many uniformed policemen wandered about.

And how odd that policemen were questioning the occupants of the pleasure and fishing boats in the marina, even searching the vessels. Perhaps someone's jewelry had been stolen?

No one in the milling crowd seemed to notice the young couple that emerged from the back of the Mercedes. The man in the white summer tux and the woman in the black evening gown blended in with the hundreds of similarly dressed couples about to board their ship.

Quinn's jaw tightened as he scrutinized the police presence. He glanced at his chronograph. Eighteen minutes left until the ship departed. Ordinarily, it would've been enough time, but what kind of delay would this dragnet bring?

Karina stood next to him in the chilly night air. He took her hand as the Mercedes drove off. "You're doing fine. This won't take long. All you have to do is smile and remember that you're Mrs. Jessica Ridgeway."

"Of course. Jessica Ridgeway. Jessica Ridgeway." She pronounced each syllable calmly, but her hand gripped his as they made their way through the crowd.

Quinn's heart rate quickened when he saw the two uniformed Russian Federation immigration officers, a man and a woman, standing behind a tall counter that blocked the only entrance to the *Sea Goddess*.

The boarding process had slowed to a crawl at the chokepoint, as the two officials scrutinized each passenger's passport, checking it against a computer whose monitor rested on a lower shelf hidden from public view.

They got into line behind a dozen other couples. Ahead of them, someone muttered, "My ship ID won't work here?"

A calm female voice replied, "Don't worry, dear. I brought our passports."

Quinn strained to hear what the immigration officials were saying and made out the male immigration officer repeating, "Next, please. You are leaving Russian Federation. Passport, please."

The minutes inching forward in line seemed like hours. Finally, there were just two couples ahead of them. The first, a young couple with a blissful newlywed look, smiled as they walked up and handed their passports to the Russian officials. The next couple, an elderly, white-haired man and his white-haired wife, waited patiently behind a rope and stanchions.

Quinn glanced at his chronograph. Nine minutes until the ship left. They were cutting it close, but all they had to do now was get past this checkpoint.

He broke out into a cold sweat when he looked up and noticed the two small cameras mounted on each side of the white awning above the immigration counter. But there was no avoiding them, especially now. They pointed directly at everyone who passed in front of the counter.

What if those cameras have some sort of facial recognition software?

He glanced at Karina. She'd done a good job with her makeup, given the limited time allotted. Nothing could be done about her facial features, of course. But even if the cameras did have facial recognition software, it couldn't process the image that quickly, within a couple of minutes.

Could it?

He looked back at the lights of St. Petersburg. Should they

turn around, slip out of the crowd and get back to the safe house?

No. There was no escape now. His plan would work. They had their passports, phony as they were. He gave Karina a reassuring smile.

The newlywed couple boarded the ship, holding hands. Now only the elderly couple stood ahead of them. The kindly looking white-haired man and his white-haired wife, surely of many years, walked up to the counter and handed over their passports.

Quinn's mouth felt dry and a curious hollowness filled his chest. Suppose they were caught? Neither he nor Karina would ever leave Russia alive. They would never live a long, peaceful life like that sensible white-haired couple. And all because of some wild scheme he'd dreamed up in a Berlin bar. Hiding in plain sight on a cruise ship!

They should've gone to ground. Gone off the grid entirely. The border between Russia and Latvia was mostly forest. They could've backpacked deep into the forest, and days later quietly crossed the border into Latvia. Now it was too late for that. What had he done?

"Next, please. You are leaving Russian Federation. Passport, please."

Quinn looked up, startled to see the male Russian immigration official waving him forward. The elderly couple was already halfway up the boarding ramp.

Karina's hand squeezed his as they walked up to the counter. He stitched a bland smile on his face and handed over their passports.

The male Russian officer handed Karina's passport to the

female officer. The male officer stared insolently at Quinn, then scrutinized his passport. He punched keys on his keyboard and looked at his hidden monitor.

Quinn glanced at the female officer. She was doing the same routine with Karina.

Both officers stared silently at their screens.

The male officer looked up. "Did you enjoy your evening, Mr. Ridgeway?"

"Yes, very much." Quinn wiped his sweaty free hand on his pants.

"And you, Mrs. Ridgeway?" spoke the female Russian officer, staring at Karina.

"Ye-Yes." Karina stammered. Her fingers tightened around Quinn's.

There was silence while the female officer gave Karina a sharp glance, then looked at her monitor. Was she waiting for Karina to say something more, to smoke her out? Quinn should've coached her on this. Would Karina freeze up if the officer asked her where she'd been that evening?

The bizarre idea flashed through Quinn's mind of leaping over the counter, taking out both officers...

"Forgive me for staring, Mrs. Ridgeway," spoke the female officer. "I was admiring your beautiful gown. Please visit Russia again. *Do svidaniya.*"

"*Do svidaniya,*" replied Karina as the officers handed both passports back to them.

Without looking back, Quinn led Karina up the entrance ramp and aboard the great ship. The engines throbbed beneath them.

At the top of the ramp, a foyer with a curving staircase in

the middle led off in three directions to hallways. To their left, music played through the open double doors of the ballroom. The music sounded friendly, so Quinn led Karina into the large, dome-ceilinged room.

Before them played a scene that could've been a grand supper club from an old Hollywood movie. In the middle of the room, a tuxedo-clad band, complete with a conductor, played a waltz. Couples swirled happily on a parquet dance floor.

To the right stood a lavish buffet table, ready for the after-theater, late-dinner crowd. An ice sculpture of a ballerina graced the center of the table, surrounded by platters loaded with crab, shrimp, lobster, and appetizers. Laughter and greetings filled the air as couples gathered around the buffet.

It all seemed beamed in from a better place, far from the killing field at the warehouse.

"I don't know how your body clock is doing, Karina, but I imagine you're hungry."

"Very much so. I have had nothing but crackers and water. But I do not like crowds. We can eat somewhere where is quiet?" The red vinyl booths behind the band were already filling with boisterous couples, and passengers had formed a line up at the bar. Karina, intimidated by the scene, moved so close to Quinn that she touched him.

"Of course." He led her to the back of the ballroom, to a secluded area of tables, and selected a table for two next to a window that overlooked the sea.

As they sat down, he heard the clanking and grinding noises of the ramp pulling up followed by the rumble of the ship's engines revving.

Several blue-and-white police boats, their light bars flashing, drifted in the water outside their window. Men on the deck of one boat shouted and waved their arms at men on the deck of another. A third police boat gave a short blast from its horn.

The *Sea Goddess* sounded its own sonorous, low-pitched horn as it slowly pulled away from the dock. They were on their way.

A waiter appeared, lit the candles, and took their drink orders. Quinn ordered a Glenfiddich on the rocks, Karina a vodka tonic. After the waiter left, Quinn smiled and glanced at Karina, looking for signs of shock or post-traumatic stress.

The opposite seemed to be taking place. As Karina looked around the great room, taking in the crystal chandeliers, the polished silver glinting on candle-lit tables, and the liveried waiters speaking in hushed tones, the white-knuckled tension she had shown at the dock seemed to melt away.

She was becoming more comfortable with her surroundings. Away from the crowds, absorbing the cheerful elegance all around, her body language relaxed and her eyes shone with curiosity.

When the waiter returned with their drinks, the *Sea Goddess* had picked up speed and cruised past the harbor. Quinn made small talk as they sipped their drinks and watched the lights of the police boats and St. Petersburg recede in the distance. Surprised by her resilience, he finally concluded that, for a small country, Latvia produced operatives of the highest quality.

When the golden lights of the city vanished into the horizon, she folded her hands on the table and looked at him as if seeing him for the first time.

"I must confess, Mr. Quinn, I had doubts about wisdom of your plan. But you have shown you are highly capable." She sipped her drink. "Is hard to believe this is real. But here we are. And are we now—"

She startled as the piercing shrieks of police sirens cut her off mid-sentence. A small fishing boat with its lights turned off sped by their window, parallel with the *Sea Goddess*. Behind it, four of the blue-and-white police boats gave close chase in formation, their light bars flashing.

The fishing boat shot past the *Sea Goddess*, its white wake frothing high in the lights of the police boats. About fifty yards past the bow of the cruise ship, the fishing boat abruptly made a splashy U-turn and then stopped, dead in the water, facing its pursuers.

The police boats quickly surrounded it on all sides, and men on the decks threw grappling hooks onto the rails of the fishing boat.

"What is that all about?" Karina watched the policemen climb onto the fishing boat as the vessels floated by.

"I believe that a woman fitting your description was reported as boarding that fishing boat. But when the police search that boat, all they'll find is a drunken old Russian fisherman who has forgotten to turn on his running lights."

She sighed as she watched the bobbing police boats recede behind the *Goddess*. "You are person who thinks of everything."

"Not everything. But I believe you were going to ask if we are finally safe?"

"I was." She turned away from the window and faced him, eyebrows raised.

"That point where the fishing boat turned around was the end of the twelve-mile nautical limit that is considered Russian territory. We are now in international waters and beyond the reach of the Russian Federation." Quinn raised his whiskey glass. "So yes, Karina, we are now safe."

For the first time since he'd met her, her lips curved up in a smile. It was the hopeful smile of someone who has completed a dark journey, but now turned the corner into the sunlight, and was ready to enjoy life. She touched her glass to his, her eyes bright with excitement.

He smiled back but suddenly was bone-tired. The adrenaline that had fueled him all night faded as his body grudgingly acknowledged the "mission accomplished" signal sent from his brain. He finished his whiskey. Its fire would keep him going down the home stretch.

Karina sipped her vodka tonic and flipped through the menu. Quinn's original plan, once he had her on board, had been to sedate her and have her sleep in his cabin. That plan was now out the window.

"For someone who's been through what you have, Karina, you're certainly handling it well."

"You have not met many Latvians?"

"Well, no." He thought of the old woman on Love Lock Bridge in Riga.

"We are a reserved people, but self-sufficient. And strong." She smiled again. "We have had to be, Mr. Quinn. I may now call you Michael?"

"Of course."

Throughout the entire mission, Quinn had thought of her as shown in that grim photo in the Berlin bar. He had memorized that photo in order to recognize her, and she had looked much the same in the warehouse. Even after her makeover in the safe house, he'd only had time to check that her appearance matched the doctored passport photo. His impression was of an efficient but cold operative, married to her work.

Now he couldn't help but notice how attractive her long brown hair looked, worn straight down in back against her bare white shoulders. Curving, high cheekbones gave her face a delicate prettiness. Up close, her fair skin was soft and smooth, and her generous lips had just the right touch of lipstick.

And those eyes. They were, he decided, a soft dove-gray with blue highlights. Even in that Berlin photo, they had been striking. Now they were strikingly beautiful.

In fact, she was beautiful anyplace he looked.

She finished her drink and set her glass on the table. "What happens next?"

"You must be tired, even if you don't feel it. After dinner, you should get some rest. Your supervisor, Helena, packed some clothes and personal items for you. I have a pretty nice suite with a separate living room and a couch that converts to a bed. I'll take the couch, and you get the master bedroom. Tomorrow morning, we dock in Riga."

Karina sat back in her chair and crossed her legs. A slit up the side of her dress showed a tantalizing glimpse of well-toned thigh. Her slim figure seemed made for the form-fitting black gown.

Outside their window, stars gleamed across a pristine black

sky. The sea was calm and quiet, as if it had always been so. Moonlight shimmered on a streak of rippling water.

In the ballroom area behind them, things had quieted down from the boisterous beginning. The band was playing a slow-dance ballad.

"I will do as you say, Michael. But I may make one request?"

"Certainly."

"Can we dance?"

"What?" He straightened up, not sure if he had heard correctly.

"Just one dance, please? I will explain."

"I'd be delighted." He pushed his chair back. *Why the hell not?*

Quinn led her onto the dance floor. The lights were dimmed, and the atmosphere had segued into a late-evening intimacy. The band ended its song, and couples waited quietly for the music to start again.

He held her in dance position as they waited for the music. Sitting at the table, he had only been able to look at her. Now he could feel her and, as he inhaled the enticing aroma of her perfume and perspiration, almost taste her. Her mouth, lips slightly parted, lingered only inches away. Slender eyebrows arched gracefully over eyes that looked at him with unconcealed interest.

His fatigue disappeared, replaced by stimulation from the whiskey and from the girl in his arms.

"Karina, you were going to explain?"

"Of course." He felt her breath on his face as she spoke. "How to say? Michael, we are from different worlds. In United

States, in your profession, I'm sure you are used to all this." She glanced around the room, and when she looked back, her eyes glistened.

"Where I grew up, we saw scenes like this only in movies. I lived in crowded apartment where heat was turned off every April. I waited in breadlines, lines for everything, and always there were shortages. Most of time we had cold water only, so we had to go to communal baths to shower.

"Something like this, so beautiful, is like Cinderella. It is unlikely I experience anything like this again. So this dance means much to me."

Quinn was about to reply when a low rumbling noise came from somewhere behind the ship. The band started into another slow ballad but stopped after a few bars as the rumbling quickly grew louder, drowning out all other sounds.

The dancing couples looked around, confused. The noise was way too loud to be anything from the ship's engines. Silverware jangled, and glasses vibrated on tables. The great chandeliers above them swayed, and their crystal prisms clinked.

The sound quickly escalated to a roar. Gasps came from the crowd as they not only heard the noise but *felt* it, hammering their eardrums and vibrating their bones. The air itself seemed to shake.

The roar rose to a grating screech, the kind that preceded an explosion. It sounded like a missile, coming right at them. Dancers covered their ears. Quinn wrapped his arms around a trembling Karina and pulled her close.

Shouts and cries rang across the ballroom as a *boom*, like a massive thunderclap, sounded directly overhead. The entire ship shuddered, caught in an invisible undertow as the pressure wave of air washed over the ship like a tsunami. Wine glasses rolled off tables and crashed to the floor.

The thunder rolled over the ship and kept going, fading as it traveled farther away, finally vanishing somewhere in the distant night sky.

For a moment, no one moved. Then busboys ran out to sweep up the broken glass, and waiters appeared with new bottles of wine. The band resumed playing, and the crowd buzzed about the strange noise.

"What was that?" Karina looked at him with wide eyes.

"A Russian SU-24 fighter jet, buzzing us at a very low height and at a very high speed."

"Why?"

Quinn was silent for a moment. *The cameras back at the dock did have facial recognition software. But the software had identified her too late.*

There was no need to explain this. The mission was over.

"Just sour grapes from the loser, Karina. We've won this battle."

Her bare back was damp where his hand held her. She was still in his embrace, her body just touching his.

He caressed her cheek. "Now, about that dance."

ALSO BY KEVIN SCOTT OLSON

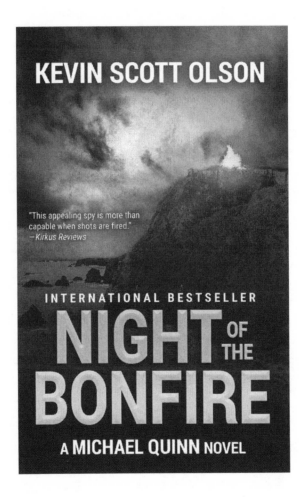

KEVIN SCOTT OLSON

"This appealing spy is more than
capable when shots are fired."
—*Kirkus Reviews*

INTERNATIONAL BESTSELLER
NIGHT OF THE
BONFIRE
A **MICHAEL QUINN** NOVEL

FOR MORE WORKS BY THE AUTHOR, PLEASE VISIT

WWW.KEVINSCOTTOLSON.COM

Made in the USA
San Bernardino, CA
21 August 2019